The Ogre's Bride

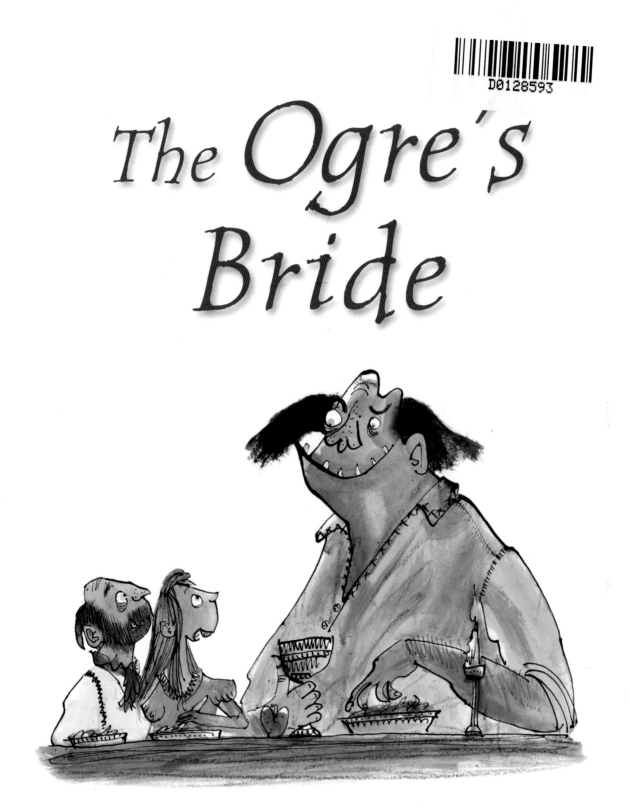

and other stories

Miles Kelly

First published in 2011 by Miles Kelly Publishing Ltd
Harding's Barn, Bardfield End Green, Thaxted, Essex, CM6 3PX, UK

2 4 6 8 10 9 7 5 3 1

Publishing Director Belinda Gallagher

Creative Director Jo Cowan

Editor Amanda Askew

Senior Designer Joe Jones

Designer Kayleigh Allen

Production Manager Elizabeth Collins

Reprographics Anthony Cambray, Stephan Davis, Jennifer Hunt

ISBN 978-1-84810-434-1

Printed in China

British Library Cataloguing-in-Publication Data
A catalogue record for this book is available from the British Library

ACKNOWLEDGEMENTS
Artworks are from the Miles Kelly Artwork Bank

Made with paper from a sustainable forest

www.mileskelly.net
info@mileskelly.net

www.factsforprojects.com

Self-publish your
children's book

buddingpress.co.uk

Contents

The Giant who Counted Carrots

A German fairytale

High upon a mountainside there was once a giant who was always very sleepy, and when he went to sleep, he would sleep for hundreds of years at a time. So every time he awoke things had changed a great deal. He spent time as a herdsman, but he did not like being poor. So he went back to sleep. On another visit he spent time as a rich farmer, but he found his servants cheated him so he went back to sleep. When he eventually

awoke again he wandered down the mountainside to see what he could see.

He came upon a rock pool where a waterfall tumbled down the rocks. A group of laughing girls were sitting dangling their toes in the water. The giant hid and watched. One of the girls was quieter than the others, but to the giant she was the prettiest. Her name was Elizabeth and she was to be married in a few days to the young duke. She and her friends chattered about the forthcoming celebrations as they paddled in the pool, and all the while the giant watched. When they skipped away, his heart grew sad. He realized just how very lonely he was.

He decided to try to win Elizabeth's heart. All through the night he worked. He covered the steep stone under the waterfall with white marble so it sparkled in the clear water. He lined the pool with silver, and filled it with darting golden fish. He covered the banks with rich green grass, planted with sweetly smelling violets and forget-me-nots and deep blue hyacinths. Then he hid himself again.

When the girls arrived they were astonished, but Elizabeth looked thoughtful. She knew that some powerful enchantment had been at work. She wandered to the edge and looked deep into the silver pool, full of the golden fish. And as she looked she heard a voice, whispering, whispering to her to step into the pool. There was a sudden splash, and as her friends looked round in alarm, Elizabeth slipped into the pool. The girls ran over to the pool and looked into the silver depths. In

vain they tried to find her. When they went home and told the young duke, he came with all haste to the pool. All the giant's adornments had vanished. The waterfall fell over steep and black rocks, the silver lining and the golden fish had disappeared from the pool, and there was not a single flower to be seen. Sadly, the duke went back to the palace and nothing would cheer him.

Meanwhile Elizabeth found herself in the giant's garden. He begged her to stay with him and be his queen, but she told him she loved the duke and would not forsake him. The giant hoped she would forget the duke, but as the days passed he saw

that she grew pale and sad. He wondered how he could cheer her, and change her mind. Then he remembered his magic staff. Whatever it touched would turn into any animal he wished for. He gave the staff to Elizabeth and for a few hours she was happy. First a kitten, then a dog, then a canary appeared thanks to the staff. But it was not long before she grew silent again.

Now the giant grew very good carrots, and he was very proud of them. He pulled up some for supper and Elizabeth said she had never tasted such delicious carrots in all her life,

which was true. So the next day, the giant took Elizabeth out into the fields round the castle where the carrots grew. As far as the eye could see there were carrots, row upon row of them.

Elizabeth asked the giant how many there were, but he couldn't tell her that at all. So she begged him to count at least one row, and as he began counting she quickly drew the staff out from under her cloak and touched a black stone that lay on the ground. It turned into a black horse with great hooves that pounded the earth as Elizabeth mounted its back and fled down the valley, away from the giant.

The very next day, Elizabeth married her duke and they lived happily ever after. The lonely giant went slowly back to his garden, and fell into a deep sleep. Many hundreds of years passed and still the giant never awoke. In time grass and plants and

trees grew over the slumbering giant, and still he slept on. Over the years the mound that was the sleeping giant became known as Giant Mountain, and so it is still called today. So beware if you see great rows of carrots on a mountain side, you might be very near a sleeping giant!

How the Rhinoceros got his Skin

By Rudyard Kipling

Once upon a time, on an uninhabited island on the shores of the Red Sea, there lived a Parsee from whose hat the rays of the sun were reflected in oriental splendour. And the Parsee lived by the Red Sea with nothing but his hat and his knife and a cooking stove of the kind that you must particularly never touch. And one day he took flour and water and currants and plums and sugar and things, and made himself one cake that

was two feet across and three feet thick. It was indeed a superior dish, and he put it on the stove because he was allowed to cook on that stove, and he baked it and he baked it till it was all brown and smelt most delicious. But just as he was going to eat it there came down to the beach from the Altogether Uninhabited Interior one rhinoceros with a horn on his nose, two piggy eyes and few manners. In those days the rhinoceros' skin fitted him quite tight. There were no wrinkles in it anywhere. He looked exactly like a Noah's ark rhinoceros, but of course much bigger. All the same, he had no manners then, and he has no manners now, and he never will have any manners. He said, "How!" and the Parsee left that cake and climbed to the top of a palm tree with nothing on but his hat, from which the rays of the sun were always reflected in oriental splendour.

And the rhinoceros upset the oil stove with his nose
and the cake rolled on the sand, and he spiked
that cake on the horn of his nose and he ate it,
and he went away waving his tail, to the desolate
and Exclusively Uninhabited Interior that is next to
the islands of Mazanderan, Socotra and
Promontories of the Larger Equinox. Then the
Parsee came down from his palm tree and put the
stove on its legs and recited the following poem,
which, as you have not heard, I will now proceed
to relate:

> "Them that takes cakes
>   Which the Parsee man bakes
>   Makes dreadful mistakes."

And there was a great deal more in that than
you would think. Because, five weeks later, there

was a heatwave in the Red Sea, and everybody took off all the clothes they had. The Parsee took off his hat but the Rhinoceros took off his skin and carried it over his shoulder as he came down to the beach to bathe. In those days it buttoned underneath with three buttons and looked like a waterproof. He said nothing whatever about the Parsee's cake, because he had eaten it all, and he never had any manners, then, since, or henceforward. He waddled straight into the water and blew bubbles through his nose, leaving his skin on the beach.

Presently the Parsee came by and found the skin, and he smiled one smile that ran all round his face two times. Then he danced three times round the skin and rubbed his hands. Then he went to his camp and filled his hat with cake crumbs, for the Parsee never ate anything but

cake, and never swept out his camp. He took that skin, and he shook that skin, and he scrubbed that skin, and he rubbed that skin just as full of dry, stale, tickly cake crumbs and some burnt currants as ever it could possibly hold. Then he climbed to the top of his palm tree and waited for the rhinoceros to come out of the water and put it on.

And the rhinoceros did. He buttoned it up with the three buttons, and it tickled like cake crumbs in bed. Then he wanted to scratch, but that made it worse, and then he lay down on the sands and rolled and rolled and rolled,

and every time he rolled the cake crumbs tickled him worse and worse and worse. Then he ran to the palm tree and rubbed and rubbed and rubbed himself against it. He rubbed so much and so hard that he rubbed his skin into a great fold over his shoulders and another fold underneath, where the buttons used to be (but he rubbed the buttons off) and he rubbed some more folds over his legs. And it spoiled his temper, but it didn't make the least difference to the cake crumbs. They were inside his skin and they tickled. So he went home, very angry indeed and horribly scratchy, and from that day to this every rhinoceros has great folds in his skin and a very bad temper.

But the Parsee came down from his palm tree, wearing his hat, from which the rays of the sun were reflected in oriental splendour, packed up his cooking stove and went away.

Under the Sun

By Juliana Horatia Gatty Ewing

There once lived a farmer who was so greedy and miserly, and so hard in all his dealings that, as folks say, he would skin a flint. It is needless to say that he never either gave or lent.

Now, by scraping, and saving, and grinding for many years, he had become almost wealthy, though, indeed, he was no better fed and dressed than if he had not a penny to bless himself with. But what bothered him sorely was that his next

 17

neighbour's farm prospered in all matters better than his own, even though he was very generous.

Now on the lands of the generous farmer (whose name was Merryweather) there lived a fairy or hillman, who made a bet that he would both beg and borrow from the envious farmer, and out-bargain him as well. So he went one day to his house, and asked him if he would kindly give him half a stone of flour to make a pudding, adding, that if he would lend him a bag to carry it, this should be returned clean and in good condition.

"Look you, wife," said he, "this is no time to be saving half a stone of flour when we may make our fortunes at one stroke. I have heard my grandfather tell of a man who lent a sack of oats to one of the fairies, and got it back filled with gold pieces. And as good a measure as he gave of oats,

he got back of gold." Saying which, the farmer took a canvas bag to the flour bin, and began to fill it.

Meanwhile the fairy sat in the larder window and cried, "Give us good measure, neighbour, and you shall have anything under the sun."

When the farmer heard this he was nearly out of his wits with delight, and his hands shook so that the flour spilled all about the larder floor.

"Thank you, dear sir," he said, "It's a bargain, and I agree to it. My wife hears us, and is witness. Wife! Wife!" he cried, running into the kitchen, "I am to have anything under the sun. I think of asking for neighbour Merryweather's estate, but I should like to make a wise choice."

"You will have a week to think it over in," said the fairy, who had come in behind him. "I must be off now, so give me my flour, and come to the hill

 19

behind your house seven days hence at midnight."

"Not for seven days, did you say, sir? Then I expect something over and above the exact amount. Interest we call it, my dear sir."

"What do you expect?" asked the fairy.

"Oh, dear sir, I leave it to you," said the farmer.

With that the fairy shouldered the flour-sack, and went on his way.

For the next seven days, the farmer had no peace for thinking and scheming how to get the most out of his one wish. His wife made many suggestions to which he did not agree, but he was careful not to quarrel with her.

And so, after a week of sleepless nights and anxious days, he came back to his first thought, and resolved to ask for his neighbour's estate.

At last the night came. It was full moon, and the farmer looked anxiously about, fearing the fairy

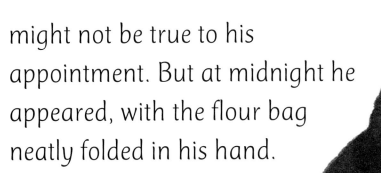

might not be true to his appointment. But at midnight he appeared, with the flour bag neatly folded in his hand.

"You hold to the agreement," said the farmer, "I am to have anything under the sun."

"Ask away," said the fairy.

"I want neighbour Merryweather's estate," said the farmer.

"What, all this land below here, that joins on to your own?"

"Every acre," said the farmer.

"Farmer Merryweather's fields are under the moon at present," said the fairy, coolly, "and thus not within the terms of the agreement. You must choose again."

But the farmer could choose nothing that was not then under the moon. He soon saw that he had been tricked, and he was angry at the fairy.

"Give me my bag," he screamed, "and the string – and the extra gift that you promised. For half a loaf is better than no bread," he muttered.

"There's your bag," cried the fairy, clapping it over the miser's head, "it's clean enough for a nightcap. And there's your string," he added, tying it tightly round the farmer's throat. "And, for my part, I'll give you what you deserve." Saying which he gave the farmer such a hearty kick that he kicked him straight down from the top of the hill to his own back door.

The Fairy Fluffikins

By Michael Fairless

The Fairy Fluffikins lived in a warm woolly nest in a hole down an old oak tree. She was the sweetest, funniest little fairy you ever saw. She wore a little, soft dress, and on her head a little woolly cap. Fairy Fluffikins had red hair and the brightest, naughtiest brown eyes imaginable.

What a life she led the animals! Fairy Fluffikins was a sad tease. She would creep into the nests where the fat baby dormice were asleep in bed

while mamma dormouse nodded over her knitting and papa smoked his little pipe, and she would tickle the babies until they screamed with laughter.

One night she had fine fun. She found a little dead mouse in a field, and an idea struck her. She hunted about till she found a piece of long grass, and then she took the little mouse, tied the piece of grass round its tail, and ran away with it to the big tree where the ancient owl lived. There was a little hole at the bottom of the tree and into it Fairy Fluffikins crept, leaving the mouse outside in the moonlight.

Presently she heard a gruff voice in the tree saying, "I smell mouse, I smell mouse." Then there was a swoop of wings, and Fairy Fluffikins promptly drew the mouse into the little hole and stuffed its tail into her mouth so that she might not be heard laughing, and the gruff voice said angrily, "Where's that mouse gone?"

She grew tired of this game after a few times, so she left the mouse in the hole and crept away to a

new one. She really was a naughty fairy.

Next she took to tormenting the squirrels. She used to find their stores of nuts and carry them away and fill the holes with pebbles, and this, when you are a hard-working squirrel with a large family to support, is very trying to the temper. Then she would tie acorns to their tails, and she would clap her hands to frighten them, and pull the baby squirrels' ears, till at last they offered a reward to anyone who could catch Fairy Fluffikins and bring her to be punished.

No one caught Fairy Fluffikins – but she caught herself, as you shall hear.

She was poking about round a haystack one night, trying to find something naughty to do, when she came upon a sweet little house with pretty wire walls and a wooden door standing open. In hopped Fluffikins, thinking she was going

to have some new kind of fun. There was a little white thing dangling from the roof, and she laid hold of it. Immediately there was a bang, the wooden door slammed, and Fluffikins was caught.

How she cried and stamped and pushed at the door, and promised to be a good fairy and a great many other things! But all to no purpose, the door was tight shut, and Fluffikins was not like some fortunate fairies who can get out of anywhere.

There she remained, and in the morning one of the labourers found her, and, thinking she was some kind of dormouse, he carried her home to his little girl, and if you call on Mary Ann Smith you will see Fairy Fluffikins there still in a little cage. There is no one to tease and no mischief to get into, so if there is a miserable little fairy anywhere it is Fairy Fluffikins, and I'm not sure it doesn't serve her quite right.

The Pot of Gold

An Irish folk tale

Niall O'Leary was sitting on a gate in the sunshine, day-dreaming quite happily, when – TIC! TIC! TIC! – he became aware of a sharp sound coming from the field behind him.

"Now what on earth can that be?" Niall wondered to himself. "It's too loud to be a grasshopper . . . and it's too quiet to be a bird."

TIC! TIC! TIC! it went.

Niall O'Leary swung his legs over the gate and

turned around. He blinked in astonishment. There in the long grass of the field was the tiniest man Niall had ever seen, no higher than his boot. The tiny man had his back to Niall, but Niall could see that he was dressed all in green, with a long white feather in his cap. A tiny leather shoe lay before him on a rock, and he was banging away at it with a tiny stone hammer.

Niall's eyes lit up. A leprechaun! A real, live leprechaun! Niall licked his lips greedily. Every tiny leprechaun had a huge pot of gold hidden somewhere. And as everybody knew, if you caught hold of a leprechaun and squeezed him tightly enough, he would have to tell you where his treasure was buried.

Quietly, Niall O'Leary got down from the gate. TIC! TIC! TIC! went the leprechaun's hammer.

Quietly, Niall O'Leary crept through the grass.

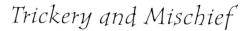

TIC! TIC! TIC! went the leprechaun's hammer.

Quietly, Niall O'Leary reached out with his large, meaty hands…

"GOTCHA!" cried Niall O'Leary, and he squeezed and squeezed the wriggling leprechaun with all his might.

"Ooooof!" cried the leprechaun. "Let me go, you big bully!"

"Tell me where your gold is and I will!" boomed Niall.

"I can't tell you anything while you're squeezing the breath out of me," the leprechaun gasped, looking rather purple.

"Oops, sorry!" blustered Niall, and relaxed his grip.

"That's better," wheezed the leprechaun, taking gulps of air. "Now put me down and I promise I'll

show you where my gold is hidden."

A broad grin spread across Niall's face as he lowered the leprechaun back down to the grass.

"A leprechaun can't break his promise!" he chuckled.

"No," grumbled the leprechaun rather crossly, "and my gold is buried under here." He leapt a few steps into the middle of the field and pointed at a clump of dandelions. "You'll need a spade, mind," the leprechaun added thoughtfully. "You'll have to dig quite a way down."

Niall's face fell. "But I haven't got a spade with me," he said, glumly. "What shall I do?"

"Why don't you tie your handkerchief around the dandelions so you don't forget where the gold is buried," the leprechaun suggested. "Then hurry back home and fetch a spade. I promise on my word of honour that I won't untie the handkerchief."

Niall's face brightened once again. "What a great idea!" he beamed. He fumbled in his pocket, brought out a rather grubby red silk handkerchief, and tied it around the clump of dandelions. It waved at him in the breeze like a cheerful  flag. "Thank you Mr Leprechaun," Niall remembered to say politely. "You've been mighty helpful." Then in a few strides, he was back over

the gate and away home, humming merrily.

As soon as Niall had grabbed the biggest spade he could find in the garden shed, he set off back to the field at once. All the way down the lane, he day-dreamed of what he would do with the gold. But when Niall O'Leary reached the gate, he stopped stone-still and his mouth hung open. He dropped the spade and scratched his head. "Well, blow me down," gasped Niall. All over the field, thousands of red silk handkerchiefs were tied onto clumps of dandelions and fluttering in the breeze. And Niall could hear the sound of leprechaun laughter floating over the grass on the wind.

So Niall O'Leary never got his pot of gold after all. But that is how he came to own the most successful silk handkerchief shop in Ireland.

The Ogre's Bride

By Juliana Horatia Gatty Ewing

There was once an ogre who kept a whole town in the grip of fear without anyone daring to challenge him. Over the years, the ogre had become very rich, and although he had huge cellars full of gold and jewels, and big barns groaning with the weight of stolen goods, the richer he grew the more greedy he became.

What he took from the people was not their biggest worry. Even to be killed and eaten by him

was not what they feared most. The worst was this — he would keep getting married and he only liked short wives. And as his wives always died very soon, he always needed new ones.

Some said he tormented his wives, some said he ate them, others said he worked them to death. The ogre only cared for two things in a woman — for her to be little, and a good housewife.

Now, it was when the ogre had just lost his twenty-fourth wife that these two qualities were joined in the daughter of a certain poor farmer. Everybody felt sure that Managing Molly must now be married to the ogre.

And sure enough, the giant came to the farmer and wanted to take Molly. The farmer did not know what to say and the ogre invited himself to supper at the farm later that week.

Managing Molly was not distressed at the news.

"Do what I ask you, and say as I say," said she to her father. First, he fetched a large number of hares, and then a barrel of white wine, on which he spent every penny he had. On the day of the ogre's visit, Molly made a delicious hare stew, and the wine barrel was set near the table.

When the ogre came, Molly served the stew, and the ogre sat down, his head just touching the kitchen rafters. The stew was perfect, and there was plenty of it. The ogre was very pleased, and said politely, "I'm afraid, my dear, that

you have been put to great trouble and expense."

"Don't mention it," said Molly. "The fewer rats there are, the more corn. How do you cook them?"

"Not one of my wives has ever cooked them," said the ogre, and he thought to himself, 'Such a delicious stew out of rats! What a housewife!'

"This wine must have cost you a great deal, neighbour," said he, drinking to the farmer.

"I don't know that rotten apples could be better used," said the farmer, "but I leave all that to Molly."

The ogre was now in a hurry to arrange the match, and asked what the farmer would pay.

"I should never dream of paying for someone to take Molly," said the farmer, boldly. "In fact, I shall expect payment from whoever takes her."

The ogre named a large sum of money, but the farmer told him to double it. Angrily he named a larger sum, which the farmer agreed to.

"Bring it in a sack tomorrow morning," said he to the ogre, "and then you can speak to Molly."

The next morning the ogre appeared, carrying a sack, and Molly came to meet him.

"There are two things," said she, "I would ask of any husband of mine: a new farmhouse and a feather bed of fresh goose feathers, filled when the old woman plucks her geese."

So, to save the expense of labour, the ogre built it himself, and worked hard under Molly's orders.

"Now for the feather bed," said Molly. When it snows, they say the old woman up in the sky is plucking her geese, and so at the first snow storm Molly sent for the ogre.

"You see the feathers falling," said she, "fill the bed with them."

The ogre carried in shovelfuls of snow to the bed, but as it melted as fast as he put it in, his labour never seemed done. Towards night the room got so cold that the snow would not melt, and the bed was soon filled.

Molly hastily covered it with sheets and blankets, and said, "Pray, rest here tonight, and tell me if the bed is not comfort itself. Tomorrow we will be married."

So the tired ogre lay down on the bed he had filled, but, do what he would, he could not get warm.

"The sheets must be damp," said he, and in the morning he woke with such horrible pains that he could hardly move, and half the bed had melted away. "It's no use," he groaned, "she's a very managing woman, but to sleep on such a bed would be the death of me."

And he went off home as quickly as he could, before Molly could call upon him to be married.